Writing for Love

Ruskin Bond is known for his signature simplistic and witty writing style. He is the author of several bestselling short stories, novellas, collections, essays and children's books, and has contributed a number of poems and articles to various magazines and anthologies. At the age of twenty-three, he won the prestigious John Llewellyn Rhys Prize for his first novel, *The Room on the Roof*. He was also the recipient of the Padma Shri in 1999, Lifetime Achievement Award by the Delhi Government in 2012, and the Padma Bhushan in 2014.

Born in 1934, Ruskin Bond grew up in Jamnagar, Shimla, New Delhi and Dehradun. Apart from three years in the UK, he has spent all his life in India, and now lives in Landour, Mussoorie, with his adopted family.

RUSKIN BOND

Selected and edited by

Writing for Love

A Collection of Short Stories

RUPA

Published by
Rupa Publications India Pvt. Ltd 2024
7/16, Ansari Road, Daryaganj
New Delhi 110002

Sales centres:
Bengaluru Chennai
Hyderabad Jaipur Kathmandu
Kolkata Mumbai Prayagraj

Edition copyright © Rupa Publications India Pvt. Ltd 2024
Introduction and selection © Ruskin Bond 2024

These are works of fiction. Names, characters, places and incidents are either the product of the authors' imagination or are used fictitiously and any resemblance to any actual person, living or dead, events or locales is entirely coincidental.

All rights reserved.

No part of this publication may be reproduced, transmitted, or stored in a retrieval system, in any form or by any means, electronic, mechanical, photocopying, recording or otherwise, without the prior permission of the publisher.

P-ISBN: 978-93-6156-824-4
E-ISBN: 978-93-6156-644-8

First impression 2024

10 9 8 7 6 5 4 3 2 1

The moral right of the authors has been asserted.

Printed in India

This book is sold subject to the condition that it shall not, by way of trade or otherwise, be lent, resold, hired out, or otherwise circulated, without the publisher's prior consent, in any form of binding or cover other than that in which it is published.

Contents

Introduction: The Literature of Love   ix
Ruskin Bond

Lil Runner   1
Harneet Kaur

Feuillemorte Dreams   7
Prabhnoor Gill

The Moon Flower   12
Hema Saju

Odds and Wins   18
Nupur Parasrampuria

Rendezvous on New Year's Eve   24
Somreeta Das

Plain Vanilla Love *Elvira Fernandez*	29
Love at the Doorstep *Riya Malik*	35
Sunflowers in the Rain *Aboli Mane*	41
Priya and Sneha *Keroline D'Cunha*	46
All for Love *Nandini Sengupta*	51
A Love Like No Other *Ria Dutta*	57
A Raindrop of Love *Suman Ray*	62
A Silence Spree *Shikha Prajwal*	68
Haripada *Urmi*	74
Idli Aunty *Varunika Rajput*	85

Just Playing the Part *Sumira*	91
Selfless Love *Pradeep Tandon*	97
Story of Summer *Aisha Iqbal*	104
Meeting Love *Anwesha Mitra*	110
Let's Forget Love *Nandhitha*	116

Introduction
The Literature of Love
Ruskin Bond

When I was twelve, I came across a copy of Emily Bronte's *Wuthering Heights*, and stayed up all night until I had finished reading it—a brooding tale of passionate love and frustrated desire; one of the great love stories ever written.

There are many kinds of love and you will find all of them in literature.

Another novel that I read as a boy was Louisa Alcott's *Little Women*, in which family and parenting love are eulogized.

Love for animals was depicted with charm and humour in Hugh Lofting's *Dr Dolittle* series. And in

Kipling's *Jungle Book* we find the love of animals for the boy Mowgli, who has been brought up by wolves. His best friends are a bear, a panther, and a serpent.

J.R. Ackerley expressed his love for a dog in *My Dog Tulip*. Read it, if you can get hold of it. And the classic, *Black Beauty*, by Anna Sewell, extols a girl's love for her horse.

Forbidden love. As a boy, I picked up a book called *The Well of Loneliness* by Radclyffe Hall. I was told it was unsuitable for children. That meant I had to read it! A heart-rending story of lesbian love, in which two women in love have to bear the hostility and censure of an unsympathetic society.

Pure and unselfish and heroic love can be found in the legends of Laila and Majnu, Heer and Ranjha, and other folk heroes and heroines in the folklore of India, Persia and other Asian and Middle Eastern countries. And Shakespeare immortalized the Latin lovers Romeo and Juliet in his unforgettable play.

Epic love can be found in Kalidasa's *Shakuntala*, and in the tale of Savitri (in the Mahabharata), in which the fearless Savitri confronts Yama, the god of Death, in her bid to save her beloved husband from the powers of darkness.

Most memorable for me is that great poem of

Introduction: The Literature of Love

sacred love, the *Gita Govinda* by Jayadeva. The twelfth-century poem celebrates Krishna as a lover. Estranged at first from Radha, he is ecstatically reunited with her, in language that is lyrical, sensuous, magical. The translation from the Sanskrit by George Keyt captures the magnificence of this great love poem:

> *'She looked on Hari who desired only her,*
> *On him who for long wanted dalliance,*
> *Whose face with his pleasure was overwhelmed,*
> *and who was possessed with Desire,*
> *Hari on whose body the waves of many changes*
> *appeared at the sight of her face,*
> *Like the Jamna in a mighty flood*
> *with its necklace of specks of foam.'*

There are over a hundred stanzas in this exquisite poem. No reading experience can be complete without it.

Ruskin Bond
September 2024

Lil Runner

Harneet Kaur

It had been raining hard. Stepping out of my one-bedroom apartment that Saturday was uneventful. Sensing a bit of a chill in the air, I put on my beloved beige jumper. Since it often felt a tad itchy, I went through the ordeal of pairing it with a ratty old T-shirt that said 'ratty old T-shirt' in a dreadful green. I quickly ate the half-burnt toast and emptied the coffee into my takeaway mug. It was a souvenir from an old flame. I hadn't thought about him in ages, but keepsakes are the little investments we make in life that don't need to be annihilated with the ending of relationships. Sure, it's an idea that could be disregarded by many.

Writing for Love

The walk to the university was magnificent due to the lush trees and the downpour. I didn't mind getting drenched in the rain. There are so many things that you stop cherishing when you become an adult. Getting drenched in the rain is one of them, I always thought. How the price tags of the clothes or shoes get larger than the goofy grin that you get after feeling the raindrops against your skin, I'll never know.

He sat there on the curb, tying his brown laces which had clearly been white once. I gulped down the coffee in my hand as I rushed past this guy, who was in his late sixties, and heard him holler, 'What's the rush, lil runner?' I looked back and passed him a smile to appear courteous but turned away instantly. With a few sips of my coffee left, I heard him stomping his way to me. 'Here! You might look for it later!' he said, handing over my pocketbook, which had somehow slipped out of my hands and fallen. 'Oh gosh! I can't believe I almost lost it. Thank you!' I said with utter disbelief. 'No problem,' he replied, flashing a smile, and sauntered away.

I didn't think of this incident again until the next morning when I picked up my pocketbook and saw a note that read, 'Volunteering at an old-age home.' I noticed an abstract runner on the cover. It brought a smile to my face. Whether it was the elegant gentleman or my silliness of not paying attention to the fact that he had called me a runner, I didn't know. It was a lovely morning with a pleasant drizzle and the petunia on my windowsill looked happier than usual.

I saw him again.

At the old-age home, he sat clad in his powder-blue shirt. I couldn't help but notice his elegance, silver locks, kind eyes and compassion while talking to people. He passed me a smile when our eyes met and went back to his conversation with his friend, who must have been in his thirties, just like me. I grew curiouser about him. After finishing the conversation, he sat there with his yellow coffee mug, staring blankly and enjoying the drizzle. Oh, so nonchalantly magnificent! I eventually took the chair next to him. That evening was effortless—we talked about everything and nothing, starting an unexpected journey. He had the most beautiful laughter I had ever heard—husky and so full of life. I found out later that he was visiting a friend.

Further meetings over the years included a lot of rainy mornings and evenings and A LOT of coffee.

It was unusual, as we both were able to find joy in life's most mundane things when together, and started despising the most extravagant things when alone. 'So, you don't want to get married someday?' he once asked with a frown, seemingly regretting his words soon after. 'You know, to someone you can spend your life with?' Passion is a risky game and I ended up saying, 'Why rush? What have you found by rushing into being born 34 years before me, you crazy old bat?!'

'Even a crazy old bat is loving company sometimes,' he said. 'My wife passed away ten years ago and for the thirty years we lived together, there was no intimacy.' 'But you have three beautiful kids,' I retorted. 'Intimacy doesn't always have to be physical, my love. Undressing out of clothes is immaterial compared to undressing emotionally and showing the warts and flaws that haunt your soul. It's something that I have done only with you, and I am so glad that you are a klutz who dropped her pocketbook that evening,' he chuckled. That conversation ended with mirth, a stunning sunset and a lingering warm feeling in my heart as I realized something.

There—right there during that sunset—I didn't

miss my windowsill, my obsessively organized room, the fur throw on my bed... I had found someone who felt like home.

Years passed. My parents stopped bickering with me over the question of finding someone or getting married. My meetings with him continued, and each one was better than the last. I was content. However, one evening, I saw him in the hospital. In bed, feeble and with bandages on his head—it was a sight unbearable and impossible to look at. 'I was being a klutz,' he explained, smiling. I looked after him in his last days. It was a relationship of love and perfect companionship. One morning, as I frantically looked for his medicines in the nightstand, he held my hand with his trembling fingers, exclaiming, 'Dying is nothing... What is worse is to not live... So what's the rush, lil runner?' And his first-ever words to me also became the last.

Why do they call it heartbreak? It is nothing like something breaking within you; rather, it's a feeling of having everything vanish from your body and life. Being left hollow and alone in a world full of strangers. Turns out, even if your day starts uneventfully, a lot can happen by the end of it. I still recall our conversations. Memories triggered by random things like his old T-shirt that I can't stop sleeping in or a piece of sourdough bread. These little routine things are keys to a secret doorway to the heavenly world of our moments together. But at the end of the day, how many keys can one safeguard?

Feuillemorte Dreams

Prabhnoor Gill

It wasn't this bad. The first time I saw her lifeless body, it wasn't bad at all. As if I knew. As if I could feel how every minute explosion that occurred in the faraway universe was soon going to transmute into a big one in our immediate vicinity. Something like the Big Bang. I guess I didn't know how soon. Or in what way, for that matter.

Her warm tiny hands were unusually cold, with little to no pulse in the wrist. I couldn't tell. I turned to her pale figure in the front seat. Even when nearing death, she looked nothing less than the 'billboard face' she sold. A giggle escaped my lips. Even in this state, she was making millions by the second. I wondered if it was her or the chaos she would leave behind that was worth all that. But for one or the other reason, she looked at peace. She had an air of calm around her. How could I turn to weeping when she looked like that?

A human heart is but a sly little thing.

To sate that petty little organ, I drove at a murderous speed. A speeding ticket was not my concern. It didn't matter—for all I cared, she could die twice, or as many times as she wanted to, but my weak heart wouldn't allow me to not try to save her at all. In the end, it turned out that her heart was weaker than mine. It had stopped beating even before I found her.

In passing, she had once told me her favourite colour—feuillemorte.

'Feuille—what? Is that even a colour?'

Gliding her fingers through my hair, she hummed gently and picked up a dried leaf off the grass blades. Twirling that shrivelled thing in her fingers with a faraway look in her eyes, she mumbled a response.

'It's the colour of dying leaves.'

She looked at the leaf as if she were looking at her lover. Bewitched and breathless. She looked at most things as if she were looking at them for the very first time—as if no one realized the lovemaking they were performing in the vestiges of her mind—as if no one could look at them the way she did.

Sometimes, I'd find her looking at me that way.

After her wake, I crumbled. I felt like a vessel which couldn't contain anymore. I cried and writhed. For her? For me? Or for the collective conscience encompassing each person who had admired her? I had no idea. I just knew that I had to cry. That I had to put an end to the endless cries that I cried in my head while everyone sobbed to their heart's content. I felt empty and heavy at the same time.

A hollow shell cannot live for long. Rushing to and fro for rehearsals, deal signings and modelling gigs as I pushed myself for the next stage, next event, next endorsement deal—next—next—next. Only briefly finding time to tear up a little, breathe in my sorrows and feel the cold clench of my heart. A fleeting reminder of a pumping organ inside my chest—warm and shallow. Still, it felt like I too had died the day she had.

During one of those rehearsals, I found a crumbled shopping list in the pocket of my washed indigo jeans. Billed ₹47,370.77 on 13 March 2023. On its back was a list of all the famous and not-so-famous museums of the world. Two very prominent signatures graced the right corner.

13 March. My face was wet by the time I finished reading. The saline water of Busan was nothing compared to the two streaks trickling down my cheeks. Those sorrows finally found a way into the open. A vessel which had brimmed past its capacity was now flowing freely without any shame. I didn't remember getting hauled into the company van or reaching the dorms at all. What I remembered was not something my counsellor would be proud of. I remembered her sweet hum when she glided her fingers through my hair. I remembered the soft music which bled through the theatre building doors as they were being opened and shut. I remembered the autumn wind picking up and caressing my clothed body into delicious shudders. I remembered turning 22 again, lying on the grass and hearing the soft murmur of students in the distance, with my eyes closed and gentle fingers in my hair. My head in her lap. I was alive again.

The list was still in my fist, and my body still writhed like a cradled baby crying for a little mercy from the pain of the past life. It felt as if I were born again—an infant. In my clenched fist was a little reminder that I had died once. A list of promises I had to keep to myself.

On 13 March, a day before her heart stopped beating, she seemed alive. Unusually so. I thought feuillemorte was finally fading out of her. Like Hanahaki, I hoped, it had found a place somewhere else. In someone else's chest. Killing them bit by bit from within for the love that was never returned.

I was wrong. It seemed to be keeping her alive instead. The Big Bang which was meant to have happened years ago happened the day after she seemed alive—truly and mercifully alive.

It's as if the whole universe saw it as she gave away her life in small packets of mercies. The packets that looked like dying leaves. Leaves that carried her dreams and landed on earth, becoming one with it.

She knew.

That day, I started looking at her the way she used to look at me.

The Moon Flower
Hema Saju

I had opted for the morning shift at the office for a month. I swapped hours with Benny so that he could manage the morning rush at his house. His wife was recuperating post an operation. Being a bachelor, the lot always fell on me.

I knew I would miss the early morning run and the sunrise, but still, I could manage to run in the evenings and savour the sunsets. I preferred to run on the beach. The packed sand by the water tested the strength of both my body and my mind. It was a lonely beach except for a few pairs of lovers who had found a safe nestling place behind abandoned fishing boats.

I met her one late autumn evening. After a few

rounds of running, I had settled down on the stone bench which had become my favourite spot to watch the sunrise and now the sunset.

'May I?'

I was caught off guard.

'This is a public place. You have the freedom to sit or walk wherever you prefer,' I said, smiling.

She smiled back and rested her slender frame on the bench. Her cloth bag was the only object that separated the two of us, marking a solid boundary. Her eyes had a glazed look as she watched the crimson evening sky sink into the deep silence of the sea. With her beside me, I felt that silence take on the shade of the blooming moon flowers.

There is a connection between those who love nature. They're bound by the unspoken appreciation of the simple yet profound beauty of nature. Beaulin was the most beautiful girl I had ever met. Not every man would've felt the same. In her ripped jeans and blue casual shirt, she blended with the sea and the sky. She wore no make-up and her hair was a tangled mess that danced to the tune of the caressing wind. She was all the colours—so bold and homely that I could soak my heart into the ebullient orange, crimson, pink, blue and all the other hues that finally turn grey and glisten as a single shade in the white of the moonlight.

We watched the moonrise. She then dipped her feet into the silver water and left without saying a word. It seemed that we lived on two ends of the same world. I didn't meet her after that. Months passed by. I have preferred sunsets to sunrises since the time I met her. I felt that Beaulin and sunsets shared the same peace and serenity.

Every evening, as I watched the sunset, I had imaginary conversations with her. After four months, I met her at the same spot. We said nothing. I was delighted to share the sunset and silence with her once again. I could hear our heartbeats merge with the sound of the waves. I am not a poet, else I would've recited how we would ride a sea lion and roll over giant tidal waves. We shared silent conversations and she might've listened to my silence telling her how much I liked her. I valued the importance of the moment.

I saw her almost every day but I hesitated to start a conversation. It seemed that she had set definite boundaries with people. I had no intention to go beyond the usual, familiar smile with which we both had begun to greet each other. Gradually, we started short conversations, chiefly about nature and the ways of the world. She had a deep understanding of everything. Our silences and differences brought us closer. After a year, we decided to get married. She wanted my parents to meet her and her folks. We all did.

'Not that they would object to Priyank. We're going to be a family. We should let them know.'

I nodded, smiling. She valued relationships. I felt lucky that we had crossed paths in life. The arrangements for the wedding were done, but sometimes, life doesn't go according to our plans. We often stand as a stranger at the doorstep of our own life's secret passages, baffled by the twists and turns it offers at the most unexpected hour.

It happened a week before our wedding. I knew there would be a reason behind her action. She was not fragile, I admit, but she was never a cold-blooded murderer who could rip apart someone's ribs. She did it to save herself from the beast. My family wanted me to back off from the pre-arranged wedding.

'Love cannot be discarded like old clothes.' I tried to make them understand.

The media addressed her as a 'survivor'. For

some others, she was a 'victim'. To me, she was and still is my precious silence and the breath of my soul. She had the courage to save herself. She is still chaste. I remember her telling a young girl who had survived a brutal rape, 'We women do not hold our chastity between our thighs. You've lost nothing. Be bold and rise from where you fell.'

I found her the best attorney in the state. Her sentence was reduced to a few years. Her work at the NGO was highly appreciated. That helped her earn the much-needed support.

We met once again in the visitors' room. Here, in the prison, she sees no sunsets and moonrises. I hold her hand as we sit across a table from each other. She holds onto my silence.

A drop of tear falls on my hand.

'It smells of the sea,' I say, suppressing my tears and kissing her hand.

'I am deeply wounded. Every inch of my body aches. I am beyond repair.' Her tears have the power to inundate my entire life.

Does she realize that my love transcends her body?

'I am always there with you.' I pat her shivering hand.

The Moon Flower

Tomorrow, we will watch the sunset and lie under the moonbow, enwrapped by the silence that surpasses all understanding. Someday, she'll bloom like the moon flowers with restored honour and dignity.

Odds and Wins

Nupur Parasrampuria

The chapel was embellished with magnificent blue orchids and delicate glasses. It was a breath of fresh air and a visual treat for everyone. It complimented the theme perfectly: when carved right, crystals are beautiful despite being fragile, much like relationships.

If you whirled around, you'd have been mesmerized by the ambience, feeling a sense of tranquillity and spirituality all around. The kind that makes you believe in the impossible.

I walked down the aisle behind our five-year-old daughter, who was gracefully bouncing in little steps as she scattered flowers and played the part of the flower girl to perfection. Even with my 31-year-old son by my side, I could not help but feel giddy with nervousness, a tingling running across my entire being.

There were only a few people we had invited to attend this sacred day, who now had heart-warming smiles on their faces, though my focus was only on one of them.

The panoramic view around us felt dull compared to the sparkle in his eyes as I stood before him. My son gently gave me a hand, while his wife had a tearful smile on her face. The warning look in his eyes, coupled with smirking curled lips, made me chuckle. But my husband-to-be took it all to heart and nodded in agreement, fully appreciating the gesture.

The ceremony began.

'I believe you have written your own vows?' the priest asked with a smile.

Harper responded, keeping his gaze fixed on me, 'We have.'

He was nervous, his shivering hands locked in mine making both of us giggle.

'Harper,' I could not help but whisper his name as my stomach gave birth to butterflies.

'Caramel, you are one beautiful woman I met.'

'You are one handsome man I do not regret crashing into.' I smiled.

'Crash? I regard that as an assault.' Harper nodded curtly, but his eyes teased me.

'You should not have called me Brobdingnagian. I am merely one inch taller than you.' I gestured with my fingers.

'It does make me look up to you every time I want to dive into your eyes. The best part is that you never allow me to look down upon you, as my eyes continually look up to catch a glimpse of you. I promise that this will never change.'

'Even if I punch you?' I raised my eyebrows.

'Definitely when you punch me. Who, after all, has the privilege to flaunt a lady wrapped in his arms who is capable of caring for both her man and herself? It is not every day when one falls for the boxing champion of the town who works in the noble artistic industry of defending themselves.'

'I promise to continue protecting our family, and especially you, when someone tries to disparage your love for cooking. Who says domestic life is solely for women when a man is an equal partner in a relationship?'

'Ah, Caramel, don't take those women's remarks

to heart. They are oblivious to the great love we feel for one another. I do not care if you wear the skirt or the pants in our relationship. I am just a little old man who loves doing domestic chores. I promise to continue to do so like I have been for the last 29 years of our life.'

'Well, I promise to never cook, even by mistake, with or without you.'

'And I promise not to give up on the hope of your learning to cook, even at the risk of burning down my kitchen.'

'Hey, it's our kitchen!' I exclaimed.

'Is it? I am the man of our house and your heart, Caramel. You cannot assume full accountability for our relationship. You manage our finances; I supervise our home. And we support one another every step of the way. I promise to continue to do so.'

'Are you certain you want to take charge of our home's flower arrangements? It is a huge responsibility.' I tried to muster a serious expression.

'Leave delicate things to me. I am, after all, more sensitive than you.' Harper winked.

'Then you leave me no option but to promise to always wipe away your tears. It is quite endearing.'

'Taking your surname is more endearing.'

'Harper, you only did that to piss off everyone. You still have time. I don't mind putting your last name after mine.'

'Not going to happen, Caramel. I would not let you strip me of the opportunity to proudly bear your surname. I have been honouring it for the last 25 years.'

I could not help but shed a tear, which Harper wiped off tenderly as we proceeded with the ceremony, allowing the bride to finally kiss her groom.

Emotions are pesky little things which tug at your heartstrings at the most surprising times. You can either use them as your strength, or regard them as weaknesses if you make a wrong choice. One always believes that a decision made with the heart can never be wrong.

Is it true?

I don't know.

What I do know is that life is a jumble of emotions, and when there is a battle between the mind and the heart, the heart often rules. I was no exception to this rule and every single day, I treasured the decision to marry and then remarry the man who loved me unconditionally and accepted me for who and how I was. He supported me while everyone else was against me having a child outside of marriage. He held my hand and gave his name to my child.

He presented me with the precious opportunity to go against everyone's wishes to create a truly meaningful partnership of equals. He did not back down from having a child in his mid-forties. Instead, he asked me to marry him again after more than two decades of being together.

Playing reverse psychology may or may not be successful, but our relationship of role reversal did emerge victorious in the end.

Rendezvous on New Year's Eve

Somreeta Das

New Year's Eve is a time to reflect on the year gone by and plan for the one that's coming. While most people spend this day with friends and family, Ria was sitting alone on the sofa in her spotlessly clean living room. She was all decked up and had exotic food in the kitchen ready to be served. She was waiting for someone. Just then, her doorbell rang and she rushed to the door. Her heart sank when she found a stranger at her door.

'I'm sorry to bother you,' he said, 'but my car broke down and my phone battery is dead. Can I use yours to call for help, or maybe you could charge mine?' Ria was annoyed to say the least. She had toiled the entire day tirelessly and wasn't in any mood to entertain him. She noticed that it was raining and the guy was drenched. While December rains are rare, they are not unheard of. She wanted to get rid of him quickly but couldn't just ignore him. She took his phone and closed the door.

Ria connected the charger to the phone and it sprang to life. Within seconds, it was flooded with notifications. She was trying to read a few when there was a call and she answered it. The guy on the other end was calling from a party that Ishan was late to. She briefed him about the situation and asked him to wait while she went out to get him. As he came in to answer the call, Ishan made a mess of the floor with his muddy shoes. Ria was furious with him and started listening to his side of the conversation to distract herself. What she could make out was that his car had broken down while he was on his way to the party. There was absolutely no chance of getting any help to fix it today, as it was New Year's Eve. But what puzzled her was that he refused to leave the car on the road by itself. His friends were probably ready to come and get him but he'd rather spend the rest of the night in his car. After he disconnected the call, Ishan thanked her for everything and left.

Ria had no more time to waste and started cleaning the mess immediately. After all, he could be here any minute now.

The loud burst of firecrackers woke Ria up. She had dozed off on the sofa. Another year had come and gone and he hadn't shown up. She dragged herself off the sofa and looked outside. The rain hadn't stopped; how were they lighting the fireworks? Her idle gaze fell on the car on the other side of the street and she suddenly remembered—he's still here? She went over to the car and knocked on the window. Ishan was fast asleep.

'Happy New Year!' she wished him when he rolled down his window.

'Thanks and the same to you.'

'Would you like to come inside? I have a lot of food left over.' Ishan was hesitant but agreed in the end. They shared an umbrella and returned to the house.

'So why won't you take a lift from your friends?' Ria was dying to know the reason. Ishan didn't reply and instead looked at his wet clothes for a solution.

'You are soaking wet,' Ria said. 'Why don't you

go upstairs. You'll find some clothes on the bed that may fit you.'

They did fit but very poorly. They were a couple of sizes larger than him. He still managed to tuck everything together and asked, 'Who do these belong to?'

'Why don't you first tell me why you won't leave the car, and then I'll tell you whose clothes you're wearing,' she replied.

'Well played,' he said, with a smile on his face.

As they got to know each other over dinner, they realized they had a lot of common interests. Ria, being a book editor, did not expect an IT professional to be so well-versed in literature. Ishan didn't expect her to be a football fan. After they finished dinner, Ishan asked if she would have another glass of wine with him. Ria agreed; she didn't want this night to end. She hadn't had a conversation like this in ages.

'The car,' Ishan began, 'was a gift from someone very close to my heart. She didn't live long enough for us to share the new life we were about to embark upon.' Ria lowered her head and said, 'About five years ago on New Year's Eve, the guy whose clothes you are wearing went out and never came back. That's why, every year...' her voice broke. He leaned in and held her hand. Neither of them had had a feeling like this in forever.

When Ishan woke up in the morning, the rain had stopped. Ria had dozed off on the sofa beside him. He picked up his phone and went outside to call his mechanic. It turned out that there was a small fault with the car battery which he was able to fix himself. He smiled at his fate and how it had brought him to Ria. He went inside and left a note saying, 'I'll be right back.' He made a quick run to the coffee shop nearby to get some food and drinks.

When Ishan came back, the house had transformed completely. It looked like nobody had lived there for ages. He kept banging on the door for Ria to let him in. His call was answered by the landlady who lived just beside the house. Ishan explained his predicament to her and she could not believe it. When she let him in, he found the place exactly like he had the previous night but everything was dusty with mould. The landlady handed him a note and said 'this is all that he had left Ria with'.

When he looked at the note, his head started spinning. 'But this is the note I left this morning.'

Plain Vanilla Love

Elvira Fernandez

'Amma, here are the curry leaves you asked for,' said Radha, the maid, walking into the kitchen.

'Wash it in the sink. Our neighbours have the most aromatic curry leaves tree,' Gayathri replied, chopping green chillies. 'Did you dice all the vegetables?'

'No, Amma, not all. The bottle gourd, red pumpkin and potatoes are done. I'll just clean the drumsticks and then cut them,' Radha said, taking up the knife.

'Don't cut them more than two inches long.'

'Okay, Amma. Appa will be very happy today. You're making his favourite dinner.' Radha turned to look at her mistress, who treated her like a daughter.

'Hmm...' Gayathri smiled as she thought of her Hari.

Hari Vishwanathan was a prosperous businessman in his late fifties—the owner of a renowned saree store in their city. In spite of being so affluent, Hari lived a life of humility. He was much admired for his friendly nature by friends and customers. Gayathri's face showed pain as she recollected the previous year, when she had nearly lost him to the deadly COVID-19 pandemic. But her Hari was a fighter! She wiped away the tear that had trickled down her cheek and smiled. He knew she had no one else except him. He had stood by her side even after all these years.

Gayathri had been widowed the very next day of her marriage—a forced marriage. She had always loved Hari, and he had loved her. But their parents were sworn enemies and wouldn't hear of it. When he insisted once again on marrying her after the death of her husband, his mother blackmailed him into promising her that he would never marry Gayathri. He did promise and then swore to never marry anyone else either. When life became hell for the young lovers, Hari convinced Gayathri to elope

Plain Vanilla Love

with him to a big city, where neither his family nor hers would ever find them. Once in the big city, Hari repeatedly insisted on marrying her but each time, she reminded him to honour his vow. They were happy together, married or not.

'Amma, shall I put the batter in the *idli* moulds?' Radha interrupted her reminiscences.

'Yes, Radha. While that gets steamed, I'll just grind this coconut chutney and prepare the sambar.' Gayathri laboured at the grinding stone. Although her kitchen was fitted out with modern gadgets, she knew he savoured the taste of handmade chutney.

'Your neighbour, Mrs Bhalla, is going with her husband to a fancy restaurant tonight. I heard her boasting to one of her friends over the phone while I was washing their utensils. She's a big show-off!' Radha said, stirring the batter in the large bowl before pouring some into the moulds. 'They'll eat butter chicken, *sarson da saag*, *makke ki* roti and what not! Why can't she cook these dishes at home? Hotels are so expensive.'

'Hmm. She likes going out,' Gayathri said, washing her hands and putting on the *haandi* for the sambar. 'Radha, just take out the milk from the fridge. We'll make some *payasam* also.'

'Yes, Amma!' Radha opened the fridge as Gayathri added the chopped vegetables to the spluttering ghee.

'Amma! You look so beautiful,' said Radha, on the brink of leaving, as she stopped to admire the woman she worshipped as much as Goddess Durga. 'This is Appa's favourite colour, isn't it?'

'He gifted me this saree for my birthday last year.' Gayathri smiled and smoothed out a crease on the pleats.

'Appa will be fully *flat* today!' Radha teased her gently as she stepped out of the front door of the small bungalow.

'*Dhat!* Naughty girl!' Gayathri blushed as she shut the door.

'Good evening!' Hari said when Gayathri opened the door before he even rang the doorbell. The wall clock in their living room struck 10.00 p.m.

'Good evening. How was your day?' Gayathri

enquired warmly, taking his old cloth shoulder bag and tiffin.

'Very good. Quite a busy day. Gayathri, wait a minute. Just give me that bag.'

'Here...' She held out the bag to him.

'I've brought something for you.' He smiled warmly.

'Really! What?'

'Your favourites—a *gajra* of jasmines and *kanakambaram*s. Shall I?'

'Yes, of course. How lovely! I love the fragrance.' Gayathri inhaled deeply as she turned around gracefully so that he could affix a string of the sweet-smelling flowers on to her high bun.

'Thank you.'

'I have something more for you,' Hari said, placing his hands on her shoulders. He turned her around and then laughed at her surprised face.

'Something more? What else?'

'Your favourite vanilla ice-cream,' Hari said. He dug into the bag and handed her the ice-cream tub.

'Oh, what a treat! Thank you so much.' Gayathri looked at him with stars in her eyes. 'I've prepared your favourite dinner.'

'I knew you would!'

'Come quickly then. I'll put out the banana leaves and warm the sambar while you wash your hands and change your clothes,' Gayathri said, walking towards the kitchen.

'Gayathri, just a minute.'

'Don't tell me you've got another surprise for me,' she said, laughing.

Hari walked up to where she stood looking at him. He clasped her shoulders gently and looked into her eyes.

'You look lovely in this pink saree. Thank you for being my lover and partner for the last thirty years. Happy Valentine's Day!'

'Hari...' Gayathri whispered, her eyes misty with tears. 'Thank you for being my *everything*! Happy Valentine's Day!'

Love at the Doorstep
Riya Malik

Fireworks lit up the dark night whilst I sat beside my grandpa, his squinted eyes focusing on the glass of whiskey in front of him. As I was young, I wanted him to talk to me. But he was strangely silent that day. So, I threw a fit and started walking away from him before he eventually called out my name. I turned around and saw his moist eyes.

'Would you like to hear a story, Tim? My story,' my grandpa asked. His voice sounded cheerful all of a sudden. I nodded, more worried than intrigued.

'Once upon a time, I was on my way to college. In those days, my hair wasn't grey, my knees were my friends, and this heart of mine was rather unbothered. Spring was around the corner, with new buds of flowers blossoming. I was waiting at the bus stop when my eyes landed on someone.'

'Who?' I asked, attentively. He smiled at my interjection.

'The most beautiful girl I had ever seen. Her hair were tickling her shoulders and her eyes looked around frantically. But her expressions... There was uncertainty clouding her face. She seemed desperate and helpless. A strange desire to protect her overwhelmed me and I approached her. With every step, my mind was busy framing the words that I was going to say to her, but when I saw her right in front of me, all the words drowned in her presence. I greeted her but my voice was startling. I stepped away from her immediately. That is when I realized that she was blind.'

My grandpa took a few long breaths, sipping from his glass. He continued, 'That's also when I noticed an engagement ring on her left hand. And that feeling, Tim... I can't describe in words what it did to me. The realization that she wasn't mine to look, hold or touch... It broke something in me that I didn't know existed.'

Love at the Doorstep

'Then what did you do, Grandpa?' I asked incredulously.

'I did what was morally right. I walked away from her. But the wind always carried her scent. The water couldn't satiate what I felt. This pang of yearning was above all else. Every prayer of mine ended with her and so would my existence, I thought. But one day, I finally saw her again. It was after months of pure purgatory. She was at her husband's funeral. Her husband was an acquaintance of my best friend, whom I was accompanying that day. May the Lord forgive me for saying this but that day, I was the happiest. This is how emotions work, Tim. They don't abide by the code of logic or ethics.'

'What did you do, Grandpa?'

'I gifted her flowers each day. Initially, she must have thought it was to express condolences for her husband's death. But as weeks passed and the flowers didn't stop coming, she must have found it strange. I used to leave them at her doorstep each morning. And she picked them up every day… Maybe because they gave her comfort just as looking at her gave me joy. Months passed but I couldn't talk to her. I was afraid of what she might say. The thought of gifting her flowers helped me get out of bed. I didn't want her to take that away from me. Until one day, she opened the door right when I was placing them on her doormat. My heart started pounding against my chest. I froze and my tongue was tied.

'That's when I heard her talk for the first time. "Perhaps I can't give you what you want, but you provide me with all that actually matters. But I am afraid that one day you will mourn the loss of all the beautiful flowers that you are wasting on me. Still, if you ever want my help in any way, I am here." That's what she said. Till this day, I remember every single word vividly. I came back home, replaying her words over and over in my head. I was excited to see her the next day. To talk to her. To be in her presence. She is going to be mine now, I thought. The next morning, I woke up to my mother's loud screams, my dad's piercing silence and my sister-in-law's suppressed sobbing. They told me my older brother got hit by a bus whilst saving a blind woman from getting run over. And in that moment, I could feel my world shattering. I knew who the woman was. It was her. There weren't many blind women in our small neighbourhood. It wasn't her fault but my family didn't think so. Then I decided I had to undo what she had done. I loved her, and I couldn't bear my family harbouring any hate towards her. So I took my sister-in-law under my wing. I married her and promised to cherish her till death do us part. I devoted myself to my family. To my wife. And promised to take care of my wife so that she could keep herself from cursing the woman I loved. One day, news came that the blind woman died of a heart attack...' A sob broke out of him.

I was eight years old when he told me this story. Twenty-eight now, I am visiting him during the holidays.

Recently, my grandpa took me out for a drive a few miles away from town. He stopped the car in front of a house. He stepped outside carrying a bouquet and left it on the doormat. He came back inside the car and a few minutes later, a woman came outside and picked them up. She smelled the flowers, closing her eyes, and a tear rolled down her cheek.

She had come here to hide from all the eyes that blamed her for her own sorrows but still desired to

Writing for Love

be seen by the man she never saw. No words were ever spoken by my grandpa, but she heard all that was to be said.

Sunflowers in the Rain

Aboli Mane

On a still June afternoon, as the grey clouds blocked out the sun and the air grew dense with foreboding, Shikha stared at the folded greeting card. A man in a coal-black blazer had left the card at the counter. Seeing it made her heart skip a beat. Her brown eyes scanned the greeting. A single sunflower was painted on the surface.

Shikha's eyes misted over as the rain pattered softly against the roof of the flower emporium. The scent of lilies, roses and tuberoses grew cloying as she stood in the middle of the displays. Bile rose to her throat. Her hands, callused and littered with tiny papercuts, some healing and others covered with Band-Aids, shook violently. Something metallic clattered onto the tiled floor. Shikha picked it up. A tag. The silver tag around his neck. She clutched it tightly within her palm. It was cold. Frigid and ruthless, much like reality.

Shikha drew a shivering breath and then, with all her might, she gripped the freshest Band-Aid and ripped it off. A streak of blood oozed from the cut. Shikha pressed open the wound. She needed to feel a deeper pain. A pain sharper than the one that gnawed at her heart.

There was an address written on the card. She wrote it down and then she burned the greeting card. As she watched it catch fire from the bright-blue lighter, all she could think of was their last interaction…

'Sunflowers?' He laughed, his grey eyes sparkling as she handed him the bouquet. Whenever the door chime jingled on a Saturday afternoon, especially close to lunchtime when Shikha would shut shop, she would know that he had arrived. Shikha closed up anyway, and the two of them often sat inside and talked. He had his strong black coffee and she her chai. That day, the afternoon sun beamed in through the arched bay windows and the scent of lavender permeated the air.

He flashed her an amused smile. 'You know, in my line of work, 'sunflowers' is a code word for death?' His face was covered in shadows as he spoke with an almost teasing lilt. Shikha paled. Her face went so white that it made him chuckle darkly.

'Don't look like that. The thrill of the chase is far better than the risk of dying.' He began to walk away. Shikha grabbed his arm. 'Wait! I am not wishing death upon you as you walk out that door! I'll give you some other flowers!' Her tone made him pause.

'Why do you care so much whether I live or die? What makes me so worth having around?' His tone was serious. The raven hair with the long sideburns that always stuck out in every direction ruffled in the breeze. Shikha had no answer. Or rather, she avoided the answer. She secreted it away, hiding it like the papercuts under the bandages. She knew her family would never approve of this man.

'Y–You are a good friend,' she answered stubbornly. 'I like all the stories you tell me. They are way more...more fascinating than this.' She gestured at the shop.

'Shikha. It is for the best that you don't get attached. A life like the one I lead is closer to suffering. I can endure it. You cannot. Best we part.'

He fumbled in his jacket pocket for a cigarette. She could read him so plainly; it was frustrating. He was conflicted. The smoke. It stung her eyes.

'I will return with another tale,' he promised as his footsteps echoed out of the door. Out of her life. Like a bird that flies away and doesn't return to roost... He was gone.

When Shikha visited the address on the card, she knew what she would be facing. The torrent battered her tired frame as she placed a bouquet on the tombstone. The heavens wept, yet she did not shed a single tear. There were no tears left. Only a sense of acrimony at the single happiness in her life being snatched away. Sunflowers. A symbol of hope and longevity. A long life. That's all she had wished for him.

She stood motionless. The rain drenched her clothes but she didn't move. The snap of the unfolding wings of an umbrella made her jolt. Someone held it over her, sheltering her from the rain.

'A rather befitting end, wasn't it?' Shikha looked up at that rather arrogant smirk on his face. Her eyes were now spitting fire.

'Was that necessary?' Her shriek was louder than thunder. He shrugged, unruffled as usual, but his expression was very apologetic. 'Sorry. I have a flare for drama. I had to stage a play to make it convincing. If you saw through it, anyone would.' Shikha glared as he scratched his head sheepishly.

'Can you forgive me? My tales end here. I don't have any more interesting stories,' he added, regarding the tomb with a new light in his eyes. They both did.

'Although, the sunflowers do add a pop of colour to my grave.' He just couldn't resist himself.

Shikha exhaled. She stood straighter.

'I hate you. Here's your stupid tag,' she mumbled, stalking forward in the rain. He followed her with the umbrella still held over her head.

'What will you do now?' They walked down the pavement like a normal couple. 'Something uninteresting. Do you have a vacancy? I am rather good at pruning flowers.' Shikha grumbled as she nudged him with an elbow. The cheek of it. The bright yellow sunflowers sodden with rain watched as the sun peeped out from behind the clouds, illuminating the sky.

Priya and Sneha

Keroline D'Cunha

'Mr Dixit, this is a case of a threatened abortion. Don't worry. We will fight to save their lives,' said Doctor Mithali.

'Her reassuring voice calms me,' said Baba, sighing.

Ours was a middle-class Maharashtrian household in Pune, where both my parents worked as scientists in government posts. Their romantic love—*eros*—conceived two foetuses in Aai's womb.

In June 1984, when Pune was reminded of having a pluviophile's heart, Aai started bleeding and was diagnosed with a threatened abortion. Baba was petrified. Aai was calmer. Her tender voice still resonates in me: 'Both of you are my fighters. Stay put.' We sensed her parental love—*storge*—brimming inside.

Aai and Baba were great devotees of Lord Ganesha. Their spiritual love—*agape*—inspired each doubtful mind. They chanted the Ganesha mantra—'*Om Vignanaashnay Namah*'—to overcome every obstacle. Courtesy the timely medical supervision and special antenatal care, Priya and I—i.e., Sneha—safely landed in the cockpit of this world. It was 9 January 1985. Bud-shaped *modak*s (sweets) were distributed. It was a state of ecstasy in the neighbourhood, as recounted in the stories we grew up hearing throughout our childhood.

Priya and I were identical twins, and we started conversing with each other inside the womb at 14 weeks. We had made the decision to survive, fight and grow up to be fighter pilots in the Indian Armed Forces (IAF). Our patriotism developed even further as we heard about Baba envisioning his twins inside Aai, swaying to the lilting melody of Doordarshan's introductory song.

When girls our age dreamt of eros, we drew planes and carved a vision board that read 'Fly to save a life.' Ours was a sisterly love—*philia*—to fly and launch rescue missions.

Writing for Love

In January 2003, we joined the National Defence Academy, Pune, to be trained as fighter pilots. The training took a toll on us, as the physical, mental and emotional stress was enormous. We stayed put to be honoured with The Best Cadet award and soon rose to the rank of Captain. We merited our places as the 'Wing Women'. That remained our collective nickname. Everything in life twinned with Priya and me. Actually, all but one.

Our 25th birthday was a milestone and we celebrated like there was *no* tomorrow.

Back then, we were based at the Bikaner-Nal Air Force station. On 10 January 2010, a day after both our birthdays, the squadron was commissioned for an air combat exercise. This was for the upcoming Republic Day parade. A regular feature that seemed irregular to me. My name wasn't on the list, so I felt rather ousted. Also, a mystifying phenomenon hovered over me. As Priya was leaving (she would soon be about 60 km from the AFS, practising an air-to-ground drill in her Jaguar fighter, the jet loaded with live armament), my airspace blurred, chest ached and eyes welled up. We hugged each other—again, like there was no tomorrow. Priya had a quirky sense of humour. She kept laughing and saying, 'Pushpa, I hate tears.' The famous line said by Rajesh Khanna in the movie *Amar Prem* (1972). She hugged me tight with even more love.

'I'll see you soon, *behna*,' were her final words and we bid adieu as thorough professionals.

At 1630 hours, my commanding officer and the flight commander, with their respective spouses, entered my room. They sat me down to break the news. 'Priya's Jaguar jet blew up in mid-air. She did not get enough time to eject.' I was frozen and torn apart. My philia had had a premonition, I sensed.

Priya's mortal remains were flown into Pune by a special IAF plane, and her final rites were performed with full military honours.

My patriotic love didn't leave my side. I had to do this for my Wing Woman. I walked as a brave soldier in front of the funeral procession, with our national flag and all her articles in my hand. The world witnessed a different love story, which was cremated inside the womb—this time, the womb was of our motherland, India. It wasn't a twin womb. She left me behind to live my life alone. It was a cremation to all the world but me. I had no closure. The loops were open-ended.

My ordeal began with sleepless nights and restless

days. I was put on medication. Aai and Baba stood by as my fighters who echoed the IAF motto every now and then: 'Touch the sky with glory.'

In my copious love for them, I catapulted into work again. Unfortunately, I was unable to step foot inside the cockpit. After a year of giving it my all, I grew tired and took a premature release from the IAF and completed my post-graduation in business studies. I never contemplated marriage. One part of me was dead. I had to resurrect it.

Time flew by and I adopted a baby girl. She was found in the debris of a dilapidated building after a 10-day search. I saw a fighter in her. We brought her home and named her Priya. Our Priya was back.

I envision my little Priya to be my Wing Woman. My storge for her will be devoted to moulding her fighter's spirit into a patriotic fighter's spirit to serve our country.

I dare to hope as I say, 'I will re-enter the space in my mother's womb where Priya and Sneha's love story blossomed. Gathering grit from there, I will step into the cockpit once again—this time, with my child, Priya. We will fly to save a life once more. *Jai Hind.*'

All for Love

Nandini Sengupta

In the early nineteenth century, an archer was exiled from the army for acts of treason. This happened in the Kingdom of Akhandi, on the periphery of the Western Ghats. The accused was not called to court and the punishment was pronounced.

Years later, one morning, there was incessant rainfall in a forest on the outskirts of the kingdom. In the open veranda of her cottage, Aranya was taking stock of her arrows. She would put them in the quiver, meticulously checking their sharp edges. Those which required a bit of work were put aside. She couldn't go out.

The next day, at daybreak, when the first streaks of sunrays had made their foray into the dense forest interiors, she mounted her pet elephant and left the cottage. Her parents were sleeping. Precariously balanced on the back of the huge species, 16-year-old Aranya rambled through the towering trees with her bows and arrows in place. Her wild matted hair fell on her eyes while she adjusted them with her soiled fingers. With her razor gaze and alert ears, she kept a strong vigil for any wild animals in the vicinity.

She was sitting by a small rivulet, washing her hands, when she heard a faint sound nearby. She thought some deer might have come up to quench its thirst in the flowing water of the stream. But as she noticed carefully, the figure was not that of any animal but of a human. His face was mostly covered with a white cloth, wrapped around his head while eclipsing his nose and jaws as well. As he removed his hide to drink water, Aranya found that he was a young man, probably in his early twenties, his cotton clothes draping his lean frame. She didn't want him to see her, so she immediately left the place with her elephant. She reached the giant banyan tree to start her practice for the day. A wooden circular plank was nailed to the tree to receive her blinding arrows.

All for Love

Two days later, while she was at the banyan tree, she could hear the sound of footsteps receding into the wild foliage. She searched for the figure but didn't find anyone. She resumed her practice for the day.

'I never knew that a girl from the jungle could also have such mastery in archery,' an unknown voice echoed in her ears.

She turned back with a look of conviction in her eyes. 'I can ride an elephant too.'

The young man was now standing in front of her, looking straight into her eyes. His lean frame belied his deep, heavy voice. Her dark eyelashes refused to blink while she was still holding the bow. She was looking at a young man in the jungle for the first time. The only other masculine form she had known was that of her father.

'You live here? I can see no one else,' the man said.

'Yes, with my parents. They live nearby in a small cottage.' Aranya indicated the direction of her dwelling with her right hand.

'Who are you? I have never seen you here before. Are you, too, banished from the stately kingdom?'

The youth was not prepared for the last part of

her question. It came as a surprise to him.

'I, indeed, belong to the palace but I have not been banished. I have come here on purpose. I must take my leave now. Will meet you soon.'

He silently disappeared into the forest the same way he had arrived. That night, Aranya couldn't sleep. Her mind was replete with curiosity and excitement about the man she had met. She kept dreaming about his small kind eyes and the movement of his lips while he was talking. All her life, she had known only her parents and the wild creatures of the dark woods. A human acquaintance was entirely new to her.

They started meeting quite often after that day. The young man would come out of nowhere, talk to her under the sun, and laugh and share stories about the palace—the King, the subjects as well as his love for his kingdom. He would hold her hand while they sat by the riverside. She would wait for him every day. Aranya wouldn't talk much about herself. Instead, she listened fondly to his tales of the land. And as Cupid sprinkled his magic, they fell in love with each other.

One day, she realized that she didn't know much about him. She only knew that his name was Prabal and that he lived at the palace. On being asked in their next meeting, he revealed that he was the Prince of Akhandi. He would soon be coronated as the new King of his land. His father had asked him to get to know his people well under the guise of a plebeian, before he took on his kingly responsibilities. Aranya was taken aback.

'I didn't know you were the Prince of Akhandi!'

'Because I never mentioned it.' Prabal put his hand gently on her face, caressing her tangled hair as it fell on her eyes.

'But I have something else to say as well. It would be my honour to have you as my life partner, and the future Queen of our land. So, if you...'

Aranya interrupted.

'I want to be a part of your regiment rather than the Queen. I love you and will continue to do so all my life. But I want to erase my father's tarnished image as a traitor from the minds of the people of our kingdom. For a long time, I have prepared myself for it. Ten years ago, he was exiled for a crime he never committed. If you truly want to honour me and believe my words, induct me into your army.'

'As you wish, my love,' he replied, looking into her eyes with deep admiration.

A Love Like No Other

Ria Dutta

It had been one month since the wedding was called off; she was so close! But destiny had something else planned for her. Following a string of failed relationships since her early teens, Anna was tired of kissing frogs, until one finally turned out to be a prince! At the not-so-ripe age of 32, she found 'the one'. Well, at least she thought she did. How was she supposed to know that he'd turn out to be a monster hiding under a hero's cape?

Crippled by depression, Anna lay under the covers every day, unable to leave the bed. She was going to start a new job soon, so she told herself she needed to get out of this rut. But she felt defeated. What was the point? She thought she could finally throw out her little black book containing the list of her many lovers over the years. But alas! It looked like her list of men was going to keep rising, while her reputation kept falling.

When you cocoon yourself with self-hate and low self-esteem, you're bound to form co-dependent relationships that go nowhere. Over the years, Anna didn't even give herself enough time to heal before she picked out her next partner, so severe was her fear of being alone. And this time too, she was preparing herself for her next prowl instead of taking some more time to heal. At this rate, she would be stuck in this vicious cycle forever.

It's true when they say we accept the love we think we deserve. Remember the movie *The Perks of Being a Wallflower*? Anna always clung to the wicked love that bad men served up and never understood the good love that the good men tried to bring into her life. Was she ever going to learn to be alone and content or grow old trying to find love in all the wrong people?

She was starting her new job soon at a small start-up that focused on pet grooming and day care. And she was hoping with all her heart that she would find her next fix there. A casual conversation, a flirty look, a ride back home...the possibilities were endless. She couldn't be alone anymore; she needed him—her next mistake.

What did the future hold for her?

'Please let it be *the one*. The man who is finally going to save me,' she prayed.

Six months later...

The sound of the alarm woke Anna from her sleep. It was 8.30 a.m. She pulled the covers closer and sunk deep underneath the warm blanket. The cold winter morning made it hard for Anna to get out of bed. She started drifting off again but suddenly thought of him and how he must be eagerly waiting for her.

The thought of keeping him waiting gave her the push she needed to get moving. She quickly got out and proceeded to get on with her morning chores. She was not a morning person but meeting him always made her want to rush out the door, no matter how early it was. It was because of him that she always made it to work on time. She didn't want to be a minute late because the sooner she got to work, the sooner she could meet him. She loved working with him. He made her day—no, he made her life light up.

She got dressed and poured herself some cereal to go. The Uber was almost here, so she grabbed her lunch and headed out the door. She plugged in her headphones and had a spoonful of cereal.

After about 40 minutes, she stepped out of the Uber and stood in front of the big black gate. The warm smile and morning wish from the salt-and-pepper-haired guard always made the day a little bit brighter. She greeted him as he unlocked the gate for her. She then stepped onto the cobbled pathway that led to her office building.

She took the first step towards the office and that's when she spotted him coming around from the back of the building. He had heard the gate open and knew she had arrived. He looked so handsome that she just wanted to run to him.

But before she could take another step, he was already running towards her. Seconds later, he jumped on her and started licking her face, his tail wagging vigorously. There he was. Snuggles, the sweetest dog she had ever met. He was the office dog and he belonged to the owner of the company.

Meeting him every morning was what Anna looked forward to more than anything else.

She had found 'the one', all right! The office romance she was so desperately hoping for. But this was better than any man. This was a kind of love she had never known or felt before. Her prayers had been answered in the best way.

Spending time with him every day made her love grow deeper in a way it had never before. Her love for him made her realize the love she needed to have for herself. And for the first time in her life, she decided to take the time to heal before she got into another relationship in a rush. She was going to be alone for as long as she needed, to really work on herself first before she let any man enter her life again. This was a scary thought but with Snuggles by her side, she felt she could do it.

She had always needed a big strong hand to hold and it got her nowhere. Luckily, when she needed a hand this time, she found paws instead and they saved her from herself, and that's all she needed to be whole again.

A Raindrop of Love

Suman Ray

The Kalboisakhi

On a lazy Saturday afternoon, as the fierce midsummer sun relentlessly rained down heat over the desert megapolis of Dubai, Sushanto woke up to a beep on his mobile phone. For a few seconds, he lay awake with his eyes tightly shut as a delicious wave of slumber rolled luxuriously through his mind and body. Finally, reluctantly, the thirtysomething Bengali in exile stretched out an arm and groped around the bed for his phone. He fished it out from under a pillow, sloppily traced out the unlock pattern and tapped open the notification. It was a text from his fiancée back in Kolkata. And it had just one word:

A Raindrop of Love

'Kalboisakhi!'

Or nor'wester—nature's increasingly rare consolation to summer-struck Kolkata. One that comes as a whirlwind thunderstorm at the end of torrid summer days, sweeping away the rabid heat with a breathless performance of light, sound and water. And then vanishes just as mysteriously as it appears.

In his comatose mind, Sushanto let out a slow sigh, and a faint smile creased his lethargic lips. His eyes still shut, his body and mind still in a state of disconnected animation, Sushanto tapped through a call to the sender, Brishti. Bangla for 'rain'. The call connected with barely a single ring.

'Not fair!'

'What, Habibi?'

'It's not fair that you get the gift of rain, while I roast here in Dubai.'

A loud chuckle erupted on the other side in Kolkata. A chuckle that sounded like an impatient waterfall gurgling down a mossy mountain side. One that Sushanto wished he had scooped up in a glass bottle and carried with himself before setting sail out of India.

'I love you... I miss you,' said Sushanto.

'Liar. You don't love Brishti. You only love the rain.'

For a moment, Sushanto wondered if his fiancée had hit home. Maybe she was right after all. Perhaps all he had loved all his life was the rain. All his love and care and longing for Brishti faded in comparison to his lifelong endless passion for the rain. Was she the one he was truly, madly, deeply and hopelessly gaga about?

'See, there you go! Lost in your endless romance for your one and true girlfriend,' Brishti complained. 'Go, get back to your dreams of Lady Rain. Call me when you finish.' The call disconnected with a beep.

The One-Night Stand

With a grin on his lips, Sushanto flipped around in his bed and let out yet another slow, lingering sigh. Outside, the incandescent sun continued to douse the cosmopolis in its white-hot rays. In his mind, Sushanto was elsewhere—on a dark and rain-soaked rooftop far, far away in his homeland. The rainstorm itself had stopped, but the soul-soothing aroma of petrichor roamed around deep in his nostrils. A cool rainswept breeze whipped around his head, and he tilted his neck up to meet this sweet embrace of his lover. Up above, streaks of lightning darted across the night sky like celestial fireworks from the mysterious heavens. Down below, the dying pitter-patter of the raindrops came as her whispered sweet nothings. The leaves of the pomelo tree next door complained in mock anger as it impatiently jettisoned the remains of the rain. The earth murmured a silent prayer of gratitude for being given relief from the day's heat, dust and agony.

The grin widened on Sushanto's face.

When She Comes to Stay

Soon, the summer would give way to monsoon. And his lady love would descend on the City of Joy with all her tempestuous might. Like a lover who has been away for too long. And yet, for all her fury, the monsoon in Kolkata had always been different from her twin sister in Mumbai, Sushanto remembered. Lady Rain had a different personality in the two rainswept cities he called home. In Mumbai, she was wild and furious. Like a scorned lover who returned to claim what she believed was hers. In Kolkata, she was mellower. Almost gentle. Like a more mature soul that caressed the city back to life after the summer's endless scorch. In Kolkata, she was a lover. Not a fighter.

She was the rain Sushanto yearned for. The kind that would descend in a melancholic pitter-patter for days on end, casting a grey gloom that took its sweet time to lift. Like an upset lover. Not that she didn't know how to seduce. The way to a man's heart, Lady Rain knew, was through his stomach. In his groggy mind, Sushanto could almost smell the aroma of a rainy day's feast wafting in from the kitchen back home: steaming hot *khichdi*, oily fried brinjals and fried fish.

Holding Hands

Sushanto wondered if his beloved rain loved him more than he ever could. She had been there at every step, every critical moment of his life. Like a guide and a friend at every crossroads.

She was there on the July day he was born. Three decades later, everybody still remembered the deluge in Kolkata the day little Sushanto had turned up, almost a month ahead of time. She was there on the day he began college. And she was also there the night he first set foot out of Calcutta. She was there, welcoming him to Delhi with a freak November shower. Like a mischievous lover splashes a fistful of water on her beloved's face.

By now, the delicious afternoon nap had all but evaporated. Sushanto got up and walked to the French windows of the precipitous balcony ledge high above the desert city. Pressing his forehead against the hot glass pane, Sushanto wondered how long before she followed him to his newest address.

'Come soon. Don't make me wait so long. It's been a while,' Sushanto found himself whispering.

A Silence Spree

Shikha Prajwal

'Did she hand him over to the police?' asked the wide-eyed little Mani.

Amma-ji threw her head back and laughed. 'No!' she said. 'Kanthi-thai started asking him questions about his whereabouts, family and troubles. The confused thief found himself responding to her. Maybe the lack of fear in her made him think that she was a social reformer or someone well-connected in society. The bewildered thief begged to be let free. But Kanthi would not let him go until she was done reprimanding and advising him. And when she began talking about helping him find a job, the thief put down his bag, folded his palms before her and ran away. We never

A Silence Spree

heard of him again.'

The kids were elated. Two of them started clapping and jumping around. Everyone else was laughing aloud.

The sudden sharp ringing of the postmaster's cycle's bell interrupted this fun.

'There is very little hope for Kanthi-thai,' Sundaranna announced as he got off his cycle and began parking it by the gate. 'Nobody could get her to talk yet.' He opened the gate, placed his slippers beside the water tap and walked towards Amma-ji. 'I haven't heard of anything like this! Who goes into a silent spree like this just due to the death of a cat? And of all the people, did it have to be Kanthi-thai, the one who talks more than she draws breath?' He touched Amma-ji's feet and sat beside her. 'They want you to visit her again, Amma-ji.'

Resting her back on one of the walls and placing her stretched legs one over the other, Amma-ji settled into her favourite spot in the veranda. The sun was setting and at this time, daily, everyone in the house eventually gathered in the large square-shaped veranda and stayed there until it was time for dinner. The cooler evenings were a welcome change after the long hot summer days.

The arrival of the postmaster coaxed the other women of the house to join in too. Sundaranna always had news and stories to share.

The mood in the veranda changed. Everyone was quiet again. As she finished folding up her betel leaf (paan), Amma-ji began shaking her head from side to side. 'If she was meant to talk, she would have by now.' She offered a betel leaf to Sundaranna, then placed one inside her own right cheek, and began speaking with her chin up to prevent spitting out. 'Talking was her way of remedying any difficult situation. Didn't she solve Chennayya's dispute with his neighbour just by talking to them? That incident had cemented her beliefs.' She now shook her head with more conviction. 'What can I say to her that will make a difference, when she has decided to abandon words altogether?'

There was silence. Everyone agreed.

'When she was younger, she once caught a rare fever.' Amma-ji recalled. 'No matter what the doctor tried, the temperature would not subside. That night, she asked me to stay with her. She was not scared; she just needed company. She began telling me about her doctor and his family and native place. Worried, I pleaded with her several times to take

A Silence Spree

rest. But she went on and on, connecting one thing to another. I remember falling asleep and waking up many times that night, only to find her talking non-stop with increasing enthusiasm. After a point, she stopped abruptly, held her chest and let out a loud burp. She said, "Rani, see, talking to you has completely healed me!" And it was true! The utterly surprised doctor told us so the next morning!' Amma-ji sighed but with a slight smile. 'This was what talking meant to her.'

There was a compassionate smile on everyone's unhappy faces. The children began to get restless. Noticing this, Sundaranna began, 'Remember that one time when Kanthi-thai wouldn't let Kishoranna go without serving him tea and snacks?' Amma-ji's face lit up, and her smile broadened into a grin as she replied, 'Hadn't he been newly posted here as a school teacher? He was young and rigid. Kanthi was just trying to be hospitable.' She laughed out loud. Sunderanna chuckled along too and offered to finish the story, saying, 'If only she had known about the state of his stomach, would she perhaps have stopped at asking about his plans for the village school! Ramanna, the gardener, still sticks to his story that when the teacher briskly walked away after declining the offer in anger, there was a wet patch on his pants that seemed to spread at a rate only slightly faster than the pace of his walk!' The children again burst out laughing, holding their stomachs and rolling on the floor.

'I must say,' Amma-ji pondered aloud, 'Kanthi-thai sometimes tends to drift into this mindless chatter that is very inconsiderate towards others.'

'Sometimes?!' Sundaranna gawked. 'She almost got me divorced!'

He began, 'Every evening, on my way home, I would ride by Kanthi-thai's house and she would be out in the garden taking a stroll. Daily, against my will, she would somehow manage to stop me for a chat and go on for at least a couple of hours. Never once was I successful in ending our conversation. It almost always used to end with her saying, "I think you must leave now, for Veena must be waiting for you," multiple times before she would finally let me go. Exhausted, I would reach home to an enraged wife who refused to believe me. Ultimately, to save my marriage, I had to figure out a new longer route to reach home earlier. But when Kanthi-thai heard of this, she was deeply pained. She came home to apologize and left after three hours.'

A Silence Spree

'Poor you,' said Amma-ji quietly. As an afterthought, she added, 'My mother used to say, "Every person is given a fixed number of breaths in a lifetime." I think my dear Kanthi has outlived her ration of words.'

Haripada

Urmi

Haripada was my father's favourite. He was his right hand—his handyman. He cleaned the grass in the courtyard of our house, fed the cows when Mother was too busy or ill, and helped my father gather the crops in bundles and load them in the barn. Father trusted him more than Mother did, and at times it created a discord between them. Mother said Haripada was a dimwit, but I sensed a hint of jealousy. He was quiet—always seen and seldom heard. In fact, he was almost like the inanimate entities in the house—essential but ignored. I guess when Providence decided to create him, He must have been careless with his speech. Haripada stammered and spoke with difficulty. I

Haripada

wonder whether that had made him a miser with words.

We never knew how old he was. In fact, I remember seeing him working around the house ever since I was aware of my existence on this planet. Yet all of us, including my elder brother and sister, called him by his name. It never irked him—nothing ever irked him, for he accepted life as it came and as it went. Like the river that flowed quietly outside the village—never complaining, never rejoicing—whose presence was only felt during its absence in the hot months of April and May. His large impassive face was hard to read. It neither revealed his feelings nor his age. His arms were muscular, probably owing to all the work he did. In his nondescript dark face, the only feature to remember was his childlike eyes.

Haripada was an orphan brought up like a destitute in his maternal uncle's house. Though his uncle was unwilling to house a child who had speech impairment and no money to his name, he had to give in to the demands of his grandparents. So, once Haripada was able-bodied and grown enough to fend for himself, he left to make his own life.

Haripada's wife was a beauty—the talk of the town. It was always a mystery how the couple ever got married. The gossip was that she had planned to run away with someone to the town, so her parents wrecked the plan and got hold of a groom of the same caste to get her married immediately. Haripada was appointed the guardian of a truant and fickle enchantress. Unfortunately, he was too mild a man to contain the wild sea. After a couple of years of marriage, she had run off with another man. Haripada was left alone.

Whether Haripada had loved his wife or not, we never knew. He was too silent to express. When she left him, he came to work as nonchalantly as before. He cleaned the garden, worked on the farm, and climbed trees to pluck palms—all just as he did on any other day. Mother asked him to dine with us at the end of the day. He sat silently in the corner of Mother's kitchen, savouring rice and dal, his calm face never betraying any feelings.

A year later, Haripada's wife returned. She was heavily pregnant. Her treacherous lover had abandoned her in her precarious condition. Everyone in the village criticized and condemned her. They asked Haripada to send her away—humiliate her and throw her away. Father was furious.

'That woman needs to be taught a lesson! The

audacity of returning to you like this!' Haripada turned a deaf ear.

'Where will she go in this condition?' he reasoned.

Though everyone fumed and seethed, though they had agitated discussions on how she ought to be poisoned, or be beaten up, or meet with some such gory end, Haripada stuck to his words. The flames of rage and anguish never seemed to touch his unperturbed soul.

She had returned on a lazy, hazy December morning. Sunlight was sparse. The village was busy with the winter harvest. In the afternoon, Haripada was, as usual, sitting in the corner of Mother's kitchen where a precious ray of sunlight had warmed up the ground, silently eating a mixture of rice and curried fish. All this while, my father was repeatedly telling him not to fall prey to his disgraced wife's plea of helplessness.

As I said, whether Haripada ever loved his wife or simply pitied her, we never knew. He never divulged his emotions, not even to my father, who was the only person he would speak to. The only time he looked anything similar to happy was when his daughter was born a couple of years after his wife had returned.

He had held the little infant in his strong arms and said, smiling, 'We shall call her Laxmi.'

Laxmi sealed Haripada and his wife Putul's marital life. At least so we thought. On his off days, he would bring his daughter and Putul's son to our pond to teach the children how to swim. On winter evenings, he would take the family for the Bonbibi mela, the annual village fair. He would buy earthen toys for Laxmi and spinning balls for the boy. Before Durga Puja, he would accompany my father to Canning, our nearest town, to buy new clothes and shoes for his family. On very hot summer afternoons, he would sit in his favourite corner in Mother's kitchen and dig his hands into our favourite summer lunch—water-soaked rice, paired with green chillies to spice up the bland platter. He would say with a content voice that he was saving up to make new rooms in his house. Now that the kids were growing, they needed more space, he'd say.

But alas, his house needed no extension. Putul left him again. Her charming and philandering lover had contacted her once more. This time, Putul ensured they got married. On an autumn evening, days after Durga Puja was over, when the mellowed-down sky makes you feel a strange sense of loss, he discovered Putul's letter written in ill-formed alphabets which said she was sorry for deceiving him but she truly loved her lover and couldn't help running away with him. She hoped he understood.

Haripada told no one of his humiliation. He came to our house as usual, worked as usual, and lunched with us as usual. Yet, in a small hamlet like ours, news never stayed in a corner. News like this spread like wildfire. Criticism and condemnation poured in like never before, this time directed at Haripada as well. Was he not man enough? How could he be such a moron? They always knew this would happen someday! They narrated stories, some true and some fabricated with the power of imagination, about how Putul was often spotted in the market indulging in her usual amorous endeavours, how they had seen Putul correspond with her lover more than once in their house on a solitary afternoon while Haripada was out in the fields and the children were at school. Some offered help. Some offered to catch the couple and teach them a lesson. Haripada, as usual, refused. He said in his usual nonchalant manner that he would like to be left alone to carry on with life.

Two months after this loss, the elder son left

as well. Whether it was because his mother's new husband was capable of providing better amenities, or whether it was because muffled whispers of his true identity kept bothering him, or whether it was simply that he wanted to be with his biological father, we never knew. But he left. Not in silence, though, like his mother. He took leave from Haripada, telling him he would like to join his mother. Haripada said nothing. He did not lament his departure. He did not ask why. He handed him a ₹100 note for the journey and told him to be careful.

We heard nothing of this departure from him. It was from Laxmi, whom mother had invited to have *puli pithe*. While Laxmi picked up the rice balls stuffed with jaggery and coconut mixture, Mother sensed her melancholy. She asked her gingerly why her brother had not come. Laxmi was unable to answer her query. Her voice choked and tears fell from her eyes unabashed. I cuddled her as warmly as I could, hoping my warmth would help diminish the coldness she felt inside.

Years passed after that winter evening. We left behind our childhood. My sister and I got married. Brother got a job in a factory near Kolkata. Father was growing old and could no longer work in the fields. He sold some of the land since there was no one to take care of them. On the remaining piece of land, he rebuilt our house and grew a vegetable garden. Haripada no longer worked. He was growing old too. He was a proud father now, and a proud grandfather as well. His daughter had studied well and taken admission for a nursing course. Mother would often quote her to tell us of the possibilities we had missed. Now, Laxmi worked in a hospital in Baruipur and her child stayed with Haripada during the day, while she and her husband were away. She only had a father-in-law, who was too old to take care of the child. Haripada often visited my father in the afternoons and helped him with the garden, plucking the lemons or watering the plants.

One sultry monsoon morning, when the sky was overcast, we huddled in the tiny shade in front of the house over warm cups of chai that Didi had just made. We were chatting, laughing and catching up on all the stories of the village we had missed while we were away. Raindrops pitter-pattered incessantly over the pond and the courtyard, making puddles and music. From the kitchen wafted the smell of fried *hilsa*. It was *Jamai Shashthi*, the annual festival where Mother pampered her sons-in-law. This time,

Father had made quite a profit from the sale of vegetables and lemons. That is why the smell of hilsa entertained us.

'Why is Laxmi not in yet?' I enquired. Laxmi was closest to my age and heart. Every year during Jamai Shashthi, Ma called her and her husband since there was nobody in her house to pamper her husband.

'She is mourning,' informed Didi, who always seemed to be better updated than I was about the goings-on in the house.

'What?! Haripada has expired?' I exclaimed, shocked. That man was so much a part of my childhood!

As it happened, it was not him but his wife instead. Laxmi spotted her in front of the hospital where she worked. She was fragile, dishevelled and dirty—in fact, hardly recognizable. Yet Laxmi somehow understood it was her. She confirmed by checking the records, which revealed that she was terminally ill with cancer. Her husband used to bring her in initially. The doctors had asked him to take her to Kolkata for better treatment. But the husband said he did not have any money. Anyway, the last time she was brought in, no one paid her bills and no one took her back either.

Haripada

The first day Laxmi saw her, she turned away in disgust. Unable to work properly during the day, she took an early leave and returned home to cry all alone. The next day, she decided to do something to prevent that disturbing picture from appearing in front of her eyes every morning. From the records, she got hold of her husband's and son's numbers. She spoke to them, urging them to take her away. The husband said he had very little money, so it was impossible for him to look after her. The son said his wife would not permit it.

All this while, Laxmi had kept the news a secret from Haripada. But when she arranged for bedding and a few clothes to make her mother comfortable, Haripada probed. When he learnt of the whereabouts of that woman who had treated him like a non-entity all her life, his first reaction was to ask Laxmi to bring her home. Laxmi looked at him in surprise. In fact, initially she was unwilling to let into their lives the woman who had broken his heart repeatedly, the one who had abandoned him. The woman who had thought of no one but herself...the cheat, the liar, the parasite who had never wavered from making use of others for her own good. Laxmi would never be able to forgive her for taking away her childhood, for the endless sleepless nights she had spent. Yet she gave in. She had to. Haripada was firm, and she had never thought of going against that one man who was a pillar in her life.

Putul died within weeks after she came in. During her last days, she seldom spoke, ate little, and just sat aimlessly in front of the main door, looking lost, forlorn and perhaps ashamed. Haripada never told her that he had missed her, or that he would miss her once she died. But every evening, he would share his paltry dinner with her and eat in silence beside her. When she died, he performed the last rites.

Then, one evening, a week after all was finished, he came to have dinner at our place. He sat in his favourite corner in Mother's kitchen and ate in silence. We never knew whether he loved Putul or not. He never spoke of anything.

Idli Aunty
Varunika Rajput

Indu continued to gaze fondly at the fluffy batter lying in the wet grinder, its faint aroma delighting her nostrils and her soul. Her lips slowly arched into an approving smile. But she wanted to be sure of the happiness simmering within. Scooping out a tiny blob of the liquid with a spoon, she placed it between her fingers and let out a euphoric chuckle. It was perfect. The perfect kind, of course, that was needed to create the perfect *idli*, the moon-like white rice cake that has stood the test of time for centuries. To Indu, making idlis was an act of love. For it demanded time, energy and patience, just like love did. And when they were being prepared for someone Indu was in love with, there was no scope for even an iota of doubt. Like today.

Transferring the foamy liquid into a big pot, she carefully covered it with a lid and placed it in the corner of her kitchen, just below the mandir—a spot fixed for batter fermentation. Only a conservative idli enthusiast from Udupi like her could believe that God's blessings were as important as fermentation in the idli-making process. She then walked out of the kitchen gleefully to answer the phone that had been buzzing for quite a while.

Her smile deepened. It was Lekha, her only daughter, who was settled in Canada.

'Hello, Chinnu!' Indu answered the call excitedly.

'Amma! Will you ever pick up my call the first time it rings?' asked Lekha, sounding irritated.

'Oh Chinnu. I did not realize. I was in the kitchen.'

'Amma, you were making idli batter for tomorrow, weren't you? Readymade batter is available online. You can always order, you know that, right? Everyone who knows you already knows you make the best idlis. Who are you competing with?' Lekha chided.

'I am not competing with anyone. Nor do I desire people hailing me for my idli-making skills. I feel happy to feed someone I deeply care about,

someone I love. Leave it, you will not understand.'
Indu felt dejected.

'Ohho, Amma! You are so innocent. I was just pulling your leg. I was worried about something else.'

'What happened to Chinnu?'

'You think that child will remember the idlis or you? Children have short memories, Amma. She is just six years old. She was four when you last met her. It has been two years. The pandemic has changed everything. I just don't want you to be heartbroken.'

Indu's smile deserted her face immediately. Her heart sank. She had been preparing idlis for Aayat's homecoming tomorrow.

Aayat was only three when the Hussains shifted to the apartment next to Indu's.

Indu, a devout Hindu Brahmin and a widow with an extremely finicky personality that found it ungodly to forge relations with people from other religions, was not particularly pleased at first to have the Hussains as her neighbours. But a three-year-old's smile is usually enough to put aside every difference. And when they hug you, that is the closest one can be to God. Indu fell in love with Aayat in no time. She would play with Aayat and treat her to many kinds of savouries. But what Aayat loved most were her idlis. Indu's chest would swell with love whenever Aayat demanded idlis. They fit into each other's lives like peas in a pod.

Unfortunately, the COVID-19 pandemic hit the world and Aayat was rendered fatherless at the young age of four. Indu tried her best to be there for Aayat and her mother, Riva. But the pandemic was a time when solidarity was to be shown from a distance. Looking at Riva's condition, her parents decided to take her home, back to Aligarh.

Indu tried to keep in touch but it was difficult considering Riva was going through a great emotional crisis. Days would go by when she wouldn't pick up the phone. By the time things normalized, Aayat was five years old and reluctant to speak to anyone over a video call. She would look at the screen, make faces and run away.

But Indu never gave up. She remained in touch with Riva.

After two excruciatingly painful years, Riva decided to resume work in Mumbai and begin Aayat's formal schooling. And Indu was the first one she called to inform.

But now, Lekha's phone call changed everything.

Idli Aunty

For Indu, Aayat had left home just yesterday. She had not considered the fact that between yesterday and today, two long years had gone by.

What if Aayat does not remember me at all? What if her tastes have changed? What will I do if she doesn't like me?

Indu suffered throughout the night.

How difficult is it to process that someone you love, and who had once loved you, may not love you anymore?

The next morning, Indu hastened towards the kitchen to check on the batter. It had risen, just as she wanted. She prepared the idlis to perfection like always and waited for Riva and Aayat.

Her heart was palpitating wildly. She had no control over it. The doorbell rang.

Indu grabbed Riva's house keys from the key holder and rushed to open the door.

There, at the doorstep, stood Riva. Beside her was little Aayat, tapping her feet.

Aayat. The apple of Indu's eyes. The reason her heart was bursting with love.

'Hello, Aayat! Do you remember me?' Indu asked softly as she went down on her knees.

The little girl looked into Indu's moist eyes and flashed a big smile. 'I know you. You are my Idli

Aunty. Have you made idlis for me?'

Indu's eyes let go of all the love they had been holding for so long.

Aayat gently wiped off the tears from Indu's face with her tiny little fingers and hugged her tight. She whispered in Indu's ears, 'Idli Aunty, I am hungry. Can we go in?'

Indu laughed and lifted Aayat up in her arms. 'Let's go, my love.'

As she shut the door behind her, Indu beamed at the thought of sharing with Lekha how love had turned her Amma into Idli Aunty. And that love had defeated all odds. Love had won.

Just Playing the Part

Sumira

What could have happened to us in another time and space? I wonder what we would be like if we weren't in love yet?

What happens now?

How do I get out of my thoughts and trust you? How do I know that I still love you?

The song 'Thrill is Gone' plays softly as Sara sips her tea by the window, lost in thoughts. The cooker whistles, notifying 5.15 p.m. Just 15 more minutes until dinner is ready. And in 15 more minutes, her lover will return home.

It's 5.29 p.m. as Sara flips her last chapatti on the *tava* and the doorbell rings.

'Welcome home! How was your day today?' asks

Sara, opening the door.

'Good but tiring,' Ajay replies, looking at the dusty patterns on the floor.

Sara's hurried steps echo chaos in the kitchen, her forehead glistening with sweat. She flips the chapatti, revealing a mild char. Disappointment flickers as she claims, 'This one is mine,' burdened with fixing everything alone.

Unaware of Sara's turmoil, Ajay seeks solace in his familiar routine. Comfortable yet weary, he retreats to his mattress, escaping the world outside and fighting the fight inside. His silent struggle mirrors the one in the kitchen.

'Dinner is ready,' says Sara.

'Coming,' replies Ajay.

In their ever-changing journey, one constant remains—sitting down to eat. Ajay instinctively reaches for Sara's hands and at that moment, they both close their eyes, immersed in gratitude and connection. They feel the familiar magic once again. Today, they still uphold the tradition but unease lingers. Ajay reaches for Sara, their fingers intertwine, eyes tightly shut, yet their hold is uncertain, like repelling magnets. Subtle vibrations fill the room, known but unseen. They seek solace in their food, diverting their attention from the unspoken truth.

'So, what's happening with you?' asks Sara.

'Nothing much. Just caught up with a few projects and two assignments that need to be done by the weekend,' answers Ajay, his eyes fixed on the morsel before him.

In more attempts to make sense out of this noise, Sara asks, 'How's the dal? Is the salt right?'

Ajay replies with an exaggerated nod, chewing the bite in his mouth, a desperate attempt to convey his appreciation for the food and, perhaps in some distant way, for her as well.

Longing to deepen their bond, they grasp for transient closeness, but words fall short, unable to hold them together. Conversation fades and efforts go in vain. And with an end to words and dinner, they share the weight of cleaning. Seeking solace in chores and then in thoughts, they retreat from the discomfort and tension that lingers between them.

Trapped in monotony, Sara pours her heart onto blank pages. *Am I so afraid of change? Can't I create my own life?* Her pen scratches the paper, drowned by deafening silence. Emotional chaos consumes her, unnoticed by Ajay lost in his phone's abyss.

Is it her distance or my inability to bridge the gap? Why

can't she love me through it? Does her love falter? What is love? Ajay's restless thumbs seek to understand their intangible connection.

As she lies on the bed and he on the couch, following a silent agreement, they both doze off with the lights still on, holding their secrets tightly in their loose and sleepy grips.

A distorted voice amplified by a megaphone abruptly shouts, 'CUT!'

In that instant, the actors shed their identities as Ajay and Sara.

'Great scene, everyone. Team, let's wrap up for the day,' the director declares, clapping alongside the entire crew.

The claps gradually subside as the voice of the actress portraying Sara rises above, remarking, 'Aren't these characters just bizarre?' She looks into the eyes of her co-actor.

The actor embodying Ajay responds, 'Yes! Indeed. They should learn to communicate. Let go of their egos for good.'

Walking towards her vanity van, the woman's thoughts continue to wander as she says, 'I can't help but wonder if love in real life is this complicated too.'

With a charming smile, the man responds,

Just Playing the Part

'Real love isn't complicated. It's the pretence that complicates things.'

'By the way, you were great today,' the actress remarks with her hand resting on the door that highlights her name on it.

'Thank you. Coming from you, that means a lot. You are always phenomenal, both on and off the set,' the actor replies with sincerity in his voice.

They communicate in a language beyond words, where dilating pupils, sweaty palms and an accelerated heartbeat do the talking.

'Hey! If you're free after the shoot, would you like to grab a cup of coffee?' she asks with a touch of sweet hesitation in her voice.

'Yes! I won't say no to that in any one of the million different lifetimes, no matter what happens,' he says while stepping towards her, away from his vanity van.

'But I must tell you that I believe romance is a hoax, in case you view our coffee date as something oh-so-romantic,' she says while inching closer towards him.

'Romance has nothing to do with love,' he responds, bridging the remaining space between them.

Breaths intertwine and eyelashes brush against each other. Freed from the script's confines, they feel something genuine. Their laughter playfully taunts the conventional images of relationships, embracing a liberation to love wholly, with or without whatever they possess and whatever they embody.

Love was always there.

They simply stepped out of the roles that denied it.

Selfless Love

Pradeep Tandon

When I reminisce about my childhood, my most vibrant, sweet and sour memories with Mangali crash into my memory lane. My rainbow of a childhood was mostly coloured by the shades of Mangali's companionship.

Mangali, our 14-year-old energetic domestic help, was six years older than me. With a wheatish complexion and average height and built, he was attractive despite the marks of smallpox on his face. Uneducated but wise, he made life interesting with his playful tricks. He affectionately called me Guddu Babu.

I loved to listen to his stories every night, but when I insisted during the daytime, he would deftly set the idea aside, saying, 'If a person listens to stories during the daytime, his maternal uncle loses his way back home.'

The celebration of Holi, a popular festival in North India, was never complete without Mangali's antics. But his escapades were not without perils. The wooden cots and window and door frames lying unattended often found their way into the Holi fire, lit on the festival's eve. *Chanda* (money) collection for lighting the Holi fire was done by Mangali and the local boys with a lot of fun and frolic. He would hide himself behind the parapet of a house's terrace, holding one end of a twine. The other end, with a hook attached, would pass over the electricity wires and dangle over the roadside. Caps or *gamcha*s (cloth towels) of passers-by would be picked up and hung on the hook, and then they would be pulled up by Mangali, only to keep them out of anybody's reach. The frenzied sounds of *bura na mano Holi hai* ('don't feel bad, it's only Holi') would echo in the air. The articles of the aggrieved person would only be returned after they had paid some chanda.

Once, Mangali threw a water balloon into a slow-moving bus that struck a schoolboy and wet his uniform. It happened two days before Holi.

Selfless Love

Enraged, the boy chased Mangali. Somehow, he managed to climb the stairs of a house and closed its terrace door. The aggrieved boy continued to bang the door while hurling the choicest abuses. After the intervention of the elders, the matter was settled.

Raw mangoes have soft seeds such that if one rubs one end of a soft seed on a rough surface, a very thin orifice emerges. If one blows air into it with their mouth, it produces a peculiar whistling sound. It is called *pipahari*. Once, Mangali was busy fiddling with his worn-out pipahari that was not producing the usual melodious sound.

'Pipahari's whistle is hurting my ears.' I pleaded with him to throw it away.

'Guddu Babu, see my aim now,' Mangali boasted.

A milk vendor carrying a milk pitcher without a lid was walking ahead of us. Mangali threw the pipahari such that it landed inside the pitcher. A maid servant coming from the opposite direction saw everything and spilled the beans. Mangali took to his heels but the milk vendor caught me instead. He came to our house and demanded money for contaminating his milk, and my mother had to pay the money.

During the hot afternoons, we would sneak off

to play with marbles in the neighbourhood, under the large canopy of a banyan tree. Mangali had great aim and could hit the targeted marble with great precision. With his help, we won all the marbles from the boys and once the game was over, we dug a deep pit under a mango tree and buried all the marbles in it.

Months later, we would dig up the pit. Sometimes, the marbles weren't there.

'Where have the marbles gone?' I asked Mangali.

He replied, 'People say that Goddess Laxmi is very fidgety. She moves wealth around. She must have moved our marbles too.'

Once, my elder brother and Mangali had a bitter quarrel and Mangali left the house in a huff. I missed him and wept, clinging on to his clothes' smell to feel him. I found a photograph of mine with him amongst his clothes. After two days, he returned to quit, but my father didn't allow him to go.

One day, I called him and said, 'Mangali, I'll teach you so that you can get a job.'

He replied, 'Guddu Babu, if I get a job, I'll have to leave you.'

That was the last time we spoke about teaching.

Later, our family shifted to Lucknow and Mangali

Selfless Love

stayed back to work with Sharma-ji, who was a dear family friend and a transporter in Moradabad. Many years passed, with life taking many twists and turns, and Mangali became a distant memory.

One day, I was in the office when my guard informed me that someone wanted to meet me. I instantly recognized him—he was my Mangali. His pale skin and wrinkled face revealed his sufferings. I continued to gaze at him and tried to come to terms with the reality in front of me.

While I was reflecting on his pitiable condition, he read my mind and spoke, 'Till Sharma-ji was there, I had all the respect, but after his death his sons threw me out of the house.'

I took care of him till he was with me. While leaving in the evening, he asked for ₹1,000 to start a tea stall. He promised to return the money once his business did well. I gave him the money and didn't say anything. He left, and I was once again lost in the rat race.

Two years later, I received a courier. The courier contained a letter, which read:

Guddu Babu, amidst all the diseases in life, shame is the most dangerous of all. I couldn't save enough earnings while managing my expenses, so I can't return the full amount to you. I am sending only ₹635. I am ashamed and not willing to show you my face.

As I count my last few breaths, I wish to recover to meet you one last time, but time and death wait for none. This cover also contains a photograph of us and an English book you once gave me. I've told someone to post the courier after my death.

By the time you get my letter, I would've left this world with the guilt of not listening to your innocent advice of becoming literate. But sometimes, love outshines logic. I'll always love you beyond logic, Guddu Babu.

With every breath, my lips quivered, my hands holding the letter trembled, my mouth dried up, and the lump in my throat grew larger. My vision became blurred as my eyes welled with tears. Some of them trickled down my cheeks and fell on the letter, moistening it. Despite being illiterate, he knew the secret of living a meaningful life through selfless love and sacrifices. Suddenly, my education seemed worthless to me.

Had I said that he didn't need to return my money, perhaps he wouldn't have been that guilty. I had feared that he might come again and ask for more money. As for him, he hadn't studied because he loved me so much. He had feared that studies might become the cause of our separation.

I couldn't convey to him before what my unsteady hands now wrote intuitively on a piece of paper.

'Mangali, I love you too, beyond any logic.'

Tears fell only to erase the words, leaving the paper blank again. Perhaps they had disappeared to reach Mangali, to convey my emotions to him.

Story of Summer
Aisha Iqbal

My favourite part of every year was the summer, when my family and I got to visit our grandparents' farmhouse on the outskirts of Bangalore. It took us a long road trip to reach there, the scenery outside slowly shifting from tapering buildings to acres and acres of green farmland. The air carried the lush smell of apples and orchids, all awash with the dull sunlight of the golden hour.

As the farmhouse came into view, my eyes darted towards the magnificent mango orchard surrounding the farmhouse. I turned back to share an excited look with my sister. Her brown hair caught the sunlight and reflected it in her deep brown eyes, making them shimmer with mysterious shapes and patterns that fascinated me.

As soon as the doors of the car opened, I jumped out, grabbed my sister's wrist and ran off at top speed to hide in one of the many mango trees around the house. Soon, we stood in front of the orchard, which seemed like a magical forest to me. I glanced at her, and she looked down at me and rested her elbow on my head, teasing me for how short I was.

'How tall are you?' she said teasingly.

'Tall enough for a 10-year-old,' I replied huffily.

When the summer breeze blew through the leaves and disturbed the mangoes, we were both hushed into silence. We stood in awe of the trees taller than both of us, looking like a fierce army ready for war against any intruders. One of the mangoes fell to the ground and suddenly, the trees seemed to unanimously agree that the two children standing in front of them were friends. We quickly picked up the fallen mango and vowed to come back first thing in the morning.

Every summer, when we came to the farmhouse, my grandparents put us to the tedious but cheery task of plucking mangoes for making jams, jellies and other scrumptious dishes.

I quite enjoyed the challenge of climbing up the trees' wide trunks. My nose was full of the smell of effervescent leaves. I enjoyed shimmying up their long, winding boughs and plucking the ripe mangoes.

The long days were filled with climbing trees, plucking mangoes and trying out sweets. An hour before sunset, my sister and I would settle down together in a hammock strung to the trees and watch the sun go down. While I would raise my hand and try to capture the light, she would laugh but hold up her own hand as well. Our linked hands looked like an open book. The rays of the dying sun illuminated the soft lines etched across our hands, and I would marvel at how they seemed to complete each other.

When the sun set, we made our way back to the farmhouse, tired from a long day. The next day, we would have to say our farewells and go back to our mundane lives once again. I hated those last days, those goodbyes after a summer full of fun and joy, but there were many more of them to come. Many summers filled with memories of childhood flew by until I arrived once more at the doorstep of the farmhouse, in another summer.

I'm not quite so little anymore; as for my sister,

she's quite a sophisticated young woman now. As soon as we stepped out of the car this time, our grandparents rushed to embrace us, exclaiming how lovely my sister was and how tall I'd grown.

'I have splendid news for all of you!' my sister announced, walking into the house.

I followed her in and she told us, brimming with happiness, that there was to be a wedding. Our parents' and grandparents' faces shone with pride, and my sister was enveloped in dozens of questions and congratulatory wishes. After they were done, I hugged her tight. She was happy, and so was I.

I awoke late the next morning, wondering why nobody woke me up, and was met with a bustling kitchen, filled with voices overriding one another. The entire household seemed to be fighting over the menu for the wedding. I quietly let myself out, not wanting to interfere.

The next few days, talks about the marriage were conducted in high spirits across the house. My sister fussed about every other thing that could possibly hinder the day. We didn't exchange many words during those days. As she was busy planning the wedding, I filled my days plucking mangoes and making jams.

Every day, not much past dawn, I would set about plucking mangoes. In the short breaks I took, I thought about the times when my sister and I used to have picnics when we were young. Looking at the trees surrounding me, I could almost see our younger selves hushing laughter and kicking up dirt, weaving our way between the trees and playing hide and seek. I thought about the marriage—how she said that in the fourteen seconds she saw him, she felt like she'd known him for fourteen years.

I thought about the fourteen years she'd known me, recalling the memories we'd made over the years—they were all tinted with sadness now.

The rustle of leaves around me whispered to me the stories of our past. The way they swayed every time I entered the orchard, welcoming my presence, made me feel happier than I'd been in a long time. They whispered to me and I talked to them. I recalled how my sister seemed to have a unique happiness in every moment, a different smile for every person. She was an open book, and I was the only one who got to write a page in it.

Now there was another person who made her smile so softly—a person who was re-writing the chapters I had so lovingly written.

Story of Summer

Yet, I didn't want to accept that this could be forever. I was scared whether I'd ever be the reason behind her smile again, or whether we'd ever be the same. I needed to revel in the memories of my past before listening to stories of the future.

So, I relived the past with the only ones who listened. The trees ready to console me and show me how the lines etched on their leaves were so similar to mine.

Perhaps they were different stories, but theirs had me in it and mine had them. Glorious as the setting sun was, all I saw were the majestic trees. The sunrays made their tops seem alight with fire, and I'd never seen a more beautiful thing. I looked at them, my eyes smiling, and said, 'As long as there are leaves on your branches, there are memories in my mind.'

Meeting Love
Anwesha Mitra

The rain had been rattling incessantly over the concrete pavement before the station gate. It was not supposed to rain at this time of the year but the weather is earth's most whimsical being.

The smell of quenched earth mixed with the greasy whiffs around had resulted in a peculiar odour. I stood there, reconsidering my decision to board the train to Whitby. My home. Or did I deserve to call it that? I had not been there in the last thirteen years.

From across the street, I saw a lady running towards the station; she paused beside me, panting.

A few damp strands of her hair were hanging

loosely on the sides of her bright face.

'I thought I missed the train. Getting a ride was difficult,' she exclaimed.

'The road seems abandoned.'

'Thunderstorms have a habit of doing that.'

'What are you doing here all alone...'

I immediately bit my tongue, worried I might have sounded rather sexist.

'You're in the clear. I didn't mind much.' Her smile was a flicker of warmth. 'Do you intend to catch the train?'

'I might,' I said.

'Great. We can wait together if you don't mind. Not familiar with this place.'

Excitement jolted me with a sudden thump in my heart. I hoped she hadn't caught me giggling.

'I would consider myself lucky.' I instantly realized that that wasn't the most charming thing to say, even though I had always been good with the ladies. She had caught me off guard. I wasn't expecting such radiant company.

I awkwardly led the way to the waiting area.

'I see you know this place?' she asked.

'I do. My father used to bring my sister and me here when we were kids.'

'Imagine if childhood came with a magic band! Wear it, and you are transported back anytime you want.'

I laughed at her words, taking the seat beside her.

'I'm not sure about that, but I would alter the past if I had such magic. Everyone would.'

'Why would anyone go through the hassle of changing the past when you have a whole future to write?'

How could she be so oblivious to the mistakes of the past? I concluded she had never made any. I was so envious of how it might feel not to have monsters of guilt clawing in the chest.

'The world appears distorted through a stained glass,' she added. 'You can never know what the real world looks like until you see it through a clear one.'

She looked at me. I was numb yet so fidgety when our eyes locked.

'Is that so?' I heard myself say.

'We look at ourselves through the glass stained with what we did in our past. Forgiving ourselves is the toughest task of all.'

Her words felt inciting. Against better judgement, they stirred me up.

Meeting Love

'But if you forgive yourself, how are you paying for your sins? Today, I was at my friend's father's memorial. She said what hurt her the most was that her father never let anyone forgive him. But how could that man not feel guilty? When the very person you despise is you, how can you let go? I am yet to understand why Hazel said that—I have seen all the wrongs her father did; how was she willing to forgive him?'

'For once, if we can keep our forgiveness for ourselves and our emotions aside, and open our hearts to let our loved ones take centre stage. Hear them out and face their emotions. You would sometimes be surprised how strikingly different they can be from yours. But first, you need to believe that you can be loved; it all starts with belief. '

We both fell silent. Even in silence, my heart was pulsating. I didn't know how true her words were, but I wanted to believe I could be forgiven for that night.

An adrenaline rush—I strived for it during those teenage years of mine. New friends and desperate efforts to fit in. We used to compete over the number of cigarettes we smoked in a day, and I had to win as a matter of ego. One night, I hid in the barn to smoke as many cigarettes as possible. I threw away the ones that were still burning. I had no idea the hay there would catch fire; the flames spread throughout the house within minutes. Jenna was in a coma for five months, and Dad almost lost his legs.

The piercing noise of the horn crushed the chain of my thoughts.

'Are you alright?' She placed a hand on my arms. I couldn't feel her touch on my skin, but I felt her warmth in my core.

We went inside the crowded train and locked the door of the dimly lit cubicle behind us.

The slow swaying of the train and the warm seats against the chilling weather slowly led us into a trance. We rested our heads back; I could sense how close hers was to mine, though I refrained from looking at her. All the same, I didn't want to stop talking to her.

'Dave Avril. I'm surprised I haven't told you my name.'

While she giggled, I felt her breath on my cheek.

'And you are?'

'Love,' she replied in a strained voice; she was falling asleep, and so was I.

Meeting Love

I looked at her, peacefully leaning on the seat, from the corner of my eye.

The noise of the crowd chattering broke my sleep. The night had ended, and so had the rain. I immediately looked beside myself, but there was only an empty seat. I searched everywhere. I assumed she might have got down.

'Where are we?' I asked a man.

'We are about to reach Whitby.'

I returned to my seat and waited for the train to take me back home. I didn't know if they would be able to forgive me, but if there was even the tiniest bit of chance, I didn't want to miss it. I could never know if it was me or if the air around me smelled like her for the rest of my journey.

Let's Forget Love

Nandhitha

It was thirty past eleven and the restaurant's usual crowd had lulled. Mahi sat in a corner waiting for her client while pretending to be a customer. 'It's a date,' he had said over the phone call yesterday. It was the third time she was meeting him, and she had still not got used to the term. People had various fancy names for their trysts but none called it a date. Ragav was definitely a unique one, out of all the clients she had had.

Mahi saw a petite girl walk towards her holding a tray that contained something that looked extremely delicious. The last time she was here, Mahi was offered a strawberry dessert; some vegetable starters were put forth the time before that.

The first time she was here, Mahi was asked what she would like to have, and she had confessed that she was not used to dining at such an elite restaurant. Ever since, Ragav had taken it upon himself to serve her what he thought she would like.

The smiling girl, whose name Mahi hadn't yet managed to learn, placed the plate in front of her and left without a word. She didn't go on with her usual, well-rehearsed speech about the dish, because that duty would soon be taken over by the man who had made the dish. Mahi returned the girl's smile rather awkwardly. From where she hailed, even a smile came with a price, and she didn't know how some could throw it around freely and randomly.

Mahi kept looking at the dish, admiring the way the yellow sauce mixed with the brown texture of what she assumed to be lamb. 'Chefs are artists in their own way,' he had told her during their first meeting. Mahi was tempted to take a bite of the delicious-looking meat but had to control herself, for she knew the chef liked giving her a thorough explanation of why everything on the plate was arranged the way it was, along with a thoughtful backstory. He enjoyed talking about food and she enjoyed listening, though not as much about food as to his husky voice.

'Good evening.'

Mahi took a long breath before lifting her head to meet his eyes, because she knew she was going to have a very hard time breathing normally when she was with him.

The walk between his restaurant and his house was something Mahi both loved and hated. She loved it because, for a brief moment, it gave her a sense of normalcy. As she walked beside him, so close to feeling him but not touching him, she could effortlessly pretend that they were in a normal relationship, and that he wasn't paying her ₹5,000 to spend the night with her. She, however, hated it for the same reason because at the back of her mind, she knew it was all pretence.

Nevertheless, the silence between them felt beautiful to her because, in her head, she filled them with words. In her mind, she asked him why he always carried the ridiculous yellow umbrella, even in the summer; why he left his watch behind at the restaurant; what perfume he used; and why he always began by kissing the side of her forehead. She also imagined a long, breath-taking kiss in a narrow lane, after which he would lift her up, carrying her in his arms all the way to his house, where they would make love, not because she needed money to pay her bills or because he needed company to forget the gruesome death of his fiancé, but simply because they were in love.

Mahi usually preferred leaving as soon as the value for money had been delivered. But with him, she loved playing house as she made coffee for both of them. She liked sipping the bitter liquid lounging in the chair in front of the bed, drenched in post-coital bliss, as he leaned on the balcony grill looking at the sleeping city.

'Will you fall in love again?' she asked.

He took his own time to turn to look at her. Her infatuation was not hidden, and so wasn't the improbability of it ever being returned by him. Her question didn't stun him. He was only perplexed by the dilemma of how to say no without giving her to believe that it had something to do with her or her profession.

Ragav borrowed time as he sipped his coffee.

'I...' he began. 'I guess not, until I see *her* again in another world.'

Mahi blinked once, and then again before the

curve of her lips broke into a barely-there smile.

The reaction bemused Ragav more than anything and his frown made it clear.

Mahi lifted herself off the chair and took slow, deliberate steps towards him. She stopped near the door of the balcony and leaned on the wall to her left.

'Good.' She nodded. 'I can have you only if she has you,' Mahi said, her face masking the emotions she was feeling. 'Your night belongs to me and my imaginings belong to you only until none of us hope to seek love back in any form.'

His eyebrows knitted. She didn't let him fathom the depth of her words as she took two long steps to shut his mind with a kiss.

That minute, she hoped the kiss transmitted some of her pain to him, so that he never healed and always needed her as a drug. Her own pain hurt less, and life became more bearable in the few hours she spent with him.